A DARK, DARK DARK CAVE

A DARK, DARK CAVE

by **Eric Hoffman**

illustrated by **Corey R. Tabor**

VIKING

The pale moon glows

as a cold wind blows
through a dark, dark cave.

Bats in flight
disappear from sight

in a dark, dark cave.

Something crawls
    up and down the walls
        of a dark, dark cave.

Shining eyes—

what occupies
        this dark, dark cave?

Giant paws
    stretch out their claws

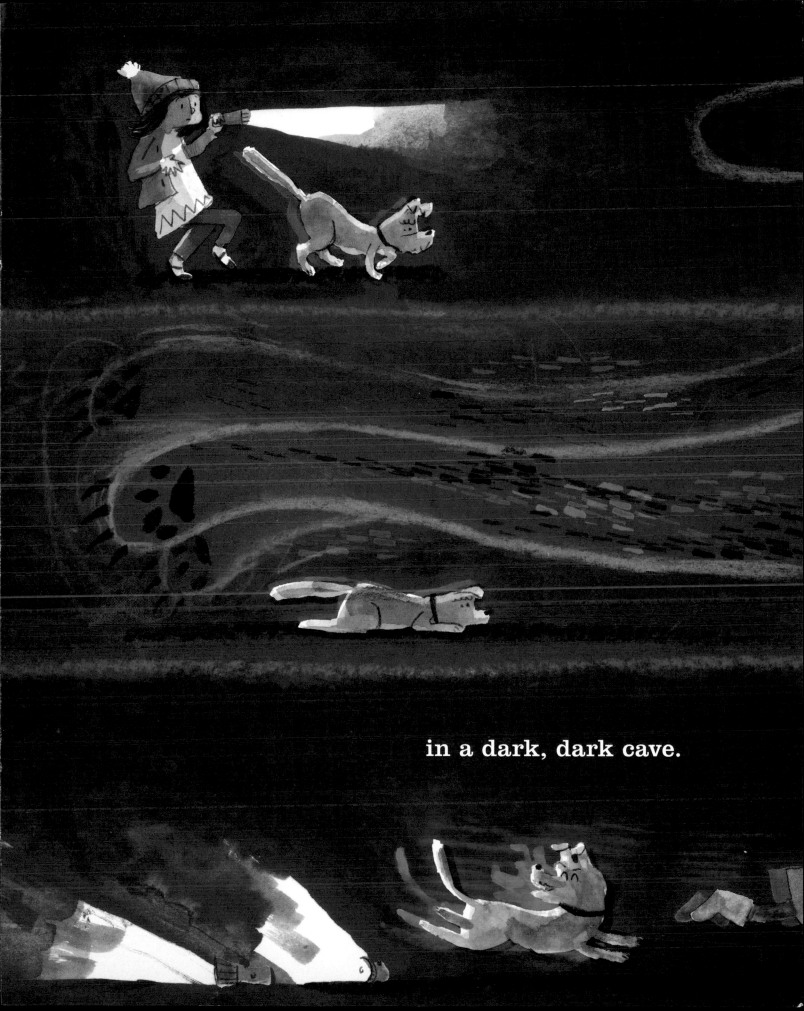

in a dark, dark cave.

Wild beasts howl
as they stomp and prowl
in a dark, dark cave.

What's that? A light!
   Who comes in sight
      of this dark, dark cave?

"Roooaaaar!"

"That's too loud, kids. Find a quiet game. The baby's sleeping."

"Sorry, Dad."

Two horses run
    in the bright, bright sun

to a blanket barn,
    wearing manes of yarn,

playing happily
    in what used to be
        a dark, dark cave.

"Ne-e-e-e-igh!"

For Sylvia and David —Eric

For Chris, Josh, and Kaylie —Corey

VIKING
An imprint of Penguin Random House LLC
375 Hudson Street
New York, New York 10014

First published in the United States of America by Viking, an imprint of Penguin Random House LLC, 2016

Text copyright © 2016 by Eric Hoffman
Illustrations copyright © 2016 by Corey R. Tabor

LIBRARY OF CONGRESS CATALOGING-IN-PUBLICATION DATA IS AVAILABLE
ISBN: 978-0-670-01636-5

Printed in China

1   3   5   7   9   10   8   6   4   2

Set in Clarendon LT Std   Designed by Kate Renner

The art for this book was created with watercolor, pencil, colored pencil, and ink and assembled digitally.